NIKI DALY has won numerous awards at home and abroad for his lyrical writing and lively illustrations. *Not So Fast, Songololo*, winner of The Katrine Harries Award and a US Parent's Choice Award, paved the way for post-apartheid South African children's books, and, with *Fly, Eagle, Fly*, is one of the Top Fifty Diversity Titles, sponsored by Seven Stories, National Centre for Children's Books, in 2014. *Jamela's Dress*, first in the bestselling Jamela series, was another milestone book, winning the Children's Literature Choice Award, the Parent's Choice Award and the Peter Pan Silver Award in Sweden. Niki's recent books for Frances Lincoln include *The Herd Boy*, *No More Kisses for Bernard* and *Seb and Hamish*, with Jude Daly. In 2009 Niki Daly was awarded the Molteno Gold Medal for his major contribution towards South African children's literature.

Nicholas
and the Wild Ones

To the Little Boy I once was

JANETTA OTTER-BARRY BOOKS

First published in Great Britain in 2016
by Frances Lincoln Children's Books
This first paperback edition first published in 2016
by Frances Lincoln Children's Books,
74-77 White Lion Street, London N1 9PF
QuartoKnows.com
Visit our blogs at QuartoKnows.com

Text and illustrations copyright © Niki Daly 2016

A catalogue record for this book is available from the British Library.

ISBN 978-1-84780-617-8

Illustrated with digital art
Set in Mr Dodo

1 3 5 7 9 8 6 4 2

Printed in Shenzhen, Guangdong, China

Nicholas
and the Wild Ones

Niki Daly

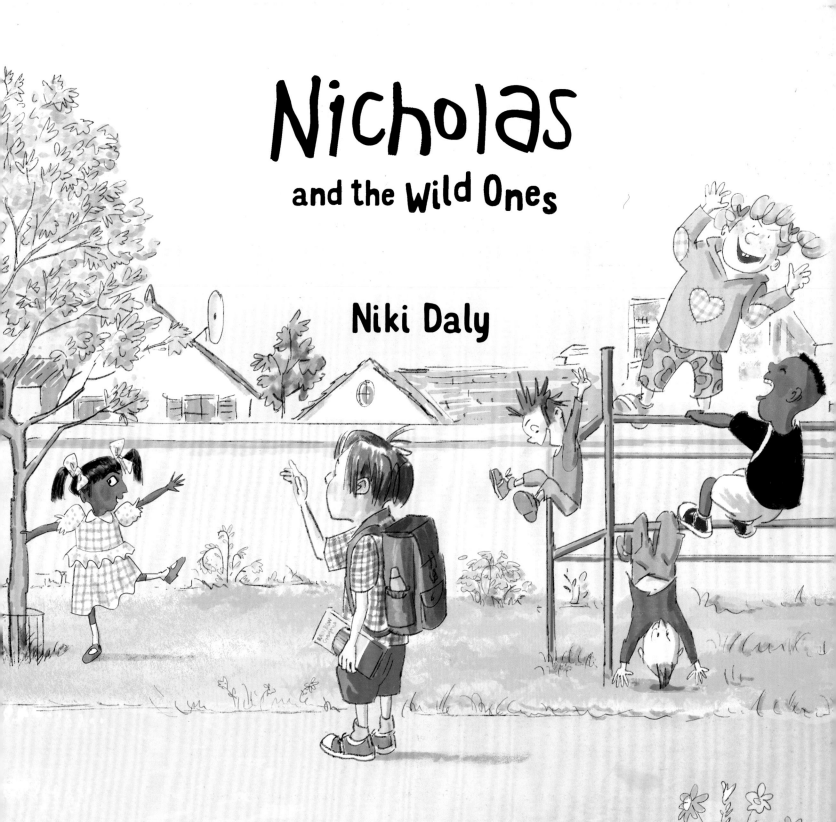

Frances Lincoln
Children's Books

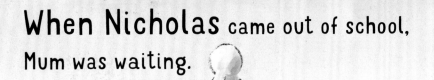

When Nicholas came out of school,
Mum was waiting.

"How did you like it?" asked Mum.
"Not one bit," replied Nicholas.
"Oh dear, why not?" asked Mum.

"See those kids over there?" said Nicholas.

"Yes," said Mum.

"Well, those are the Wild Ones," said Nicholas.

Going home, Nicholas told
Mum all about the Wild Ones.

"Charlie's the wildest," explained Nicholas.
"He stands on top of the climbing frame
and jumps on anyone who passes below him."

"That's dangerous," said Mum.

"**Lethal!**" said Nicholas. "But you know who's really creepy?"

"Tell me," said Mum.

"Wedgie Reggie," said Nicholas.
"He thinks it's very funny to yank kids
up by their underpants.
And you know what?"

"What?" asked Mum.
"My friend Stephen had to walk
around with his underpants
up his bottom."
"That's not very funny," said Mum.

"It's **mean**," said Nicholas. "But Big-Mouth Jake's even worse."
"Why?" asked Mum.

"At break, he snatched Shakira's snack and stuffed it in his mouth. He didn't even close his mouth. You could see the goo going round and round like cement in a cement mixer."

"Gross," said Mum.
"**Mega gross,**" said Nicholas.

"But now I'm going to tell you about the
SCARIEST, WILDEST ONE IN THE ENTIRE WORLD!"
"Who's that?" asked Mum.

"Cindy Crocker.
She's as **big** as a wrestler.

She pushed me from behind while I was
showing Shakira my poo-powered
motor-car invention," said Nicholas.

"That's bullying," said Mum. "Did you tell Miss Pinkerton?"
"Yes," said Nicholas. "And you know what she did?"
"What?" asked Mum.

"After break she read us a book about our rights. And NOBODY has the right to be horrid to us," said Nicholas.

"Quite right," said Mum.

"So, I won't be going to school any more," said Nicholas.

When Dad heard about the Wild Ones, he said, "You've got to show them that you're not afraid."

"How?" asked Nicholas.

"By putting up your fists like SO," said Gramps.

"No, no," said Gran. "Nicholas is an 'ideas man'. He'll think of a creative way to handle those Wild Ones."

"Yes," said Mum. "I'm sure you'll come up with a plan. But you've got to go to school. Otherwise, how will you become a famous inventor?"

So the next day Nicholas went to school –

and the Wild Ones were waiting for him.

Nicholas showed them he was not afraid
and put up his fists like SO!
This made the Wild Ones fall about with laughter.

So in art class, when Miss Pinkerton asked them all to draw something from their imagination, Nicholas drew a *Wild Ones Munching Machine.*

Shakira drew herself on a tightrope balancing on one foot!

Cindy Crocker drew a wobbly heart and coloured it pink. The rest of the Wild Ones didn't know what to draw. Instead, they laughed at Cindy's pink wobbly heart, which made big tears plop out of her eyes.

"Cindy, dear," said Miss Pinkerton, "come and sit next to Nicholas."

"That's a cool pink wobbly heart," said Nicholas.

Miss Pinkerton was happy to see Cindy and Nicholas talking to each other at last.

Uh-oh!

At break, Charlie
jumped on Nicholas...

Reggie gave him
a savage wedgie...

Big-Mouth Jake ran away
with his packet of
Space Snacks ...

Then Cindy Crocker cornered him in the toy shed and ...

this is what she said.

"Can I come and play at your house?"

"Sure," said Nicholas.

After school, Mum was pleased
to see that Nicholas had made
a new friend.

"This is Cindy Crocker," he said
to Mum.

"This is my mum," he said
to Cindy Crocker.

That afternoon they had a really fun time.

Cindy showed Nicholas how to do a powerslam.

And Nicholas demonstrated his latest
solar-powered helicopter design in flight.

When the rest of the Wild Ones
heard about Nicholas's
cool helicopter design
they all wanted one.

So in art class he showed them
how to make their own.

And **that** meant...

Charlie didn't jump on anyone,

Reggie cut out
the wedgies,

Big-Mouth Jake
didn't even think
of treats.

Cindy thought of giving
Shakira a push, but didn't,

and **this** meant ...

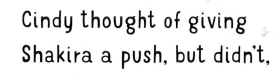

Shakira could show Nicholas how to balance
on one leg and make his eyes go like SO,

and Nicholas could show Shakira
how to hold her fists like SO.
Just in case the Wild Ones
ever turned wild again,
which they hardly ever did ...

except some days, when they simply
HAD to be wild!

And that gave
Nicholas a new
idea ...

OTHER TITLES BY NIKI DALY FROM FRANCES LINCOLN CHILDREN'S BOOKS

Seb and Hamish
By Jude and Niki Daly

Seb and Mama go to visit Mrs Kenny, but there's a dog called Hamish at the house too. *Woof woof*, says Hamish. "Home," says Seb in a little voice. While Mama and Mrs Kenny have tea, Hamish is shut in another room and Seb plays with his train set. He gets so absorbed he forgets all about Hamish – until a piece of his cookie slips under the door. Seb puts his finger through the gap, peeps under the door, and two gentle eyes look back at him...

"A charming story" – *Independent on Sunday*

ISBN 978-1-84780-602-4

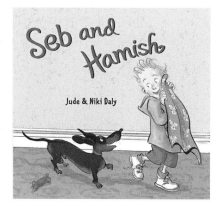

Thank you, Jackson
By Niki and Jude Daly

Every week, Jackson the donkey carries vegetables up the hill to market. But one day Jackson just stops, halfway up the hill. The farmer pushes him, pulls him, shouts at him, but Jackson WILL NOT BUDGE. Just as the farmer is about to beat his donkey, little Goodwill comes running. Quickly he whispers something in the donkey's ear – and, straightaway, the old donkey gets to his feet. The farmer is astonished. What could be the secret of the boy's message?

"Jude's famously intricate illustrations provide a feast for the eyes" – *The Independent*

ISBN 978-1-84780-484-6

Fly, Eagle, Fly!
Retold by Christopher Gregorowski, illustrated by Niki Daly, with a foreword from Desmond Tutu

When a baby eagle is blown from its nest, a farmer raises it with his chickens. But will this eagle be forever limited to life in the farmyard or will it learn to follow its destiny in the skies?

With a foreword by Archbishop Desmond Tutu this dramatically told African story will inspire children everywhere to "lift off and soar".

"A superb inspirational picture book" – *Publishers Weekly*

ISBN 978-0-71121-730-0

Frances Lincoln titles are available from all good bookshops.
You can also buy books and find out more about your favourite titles,
authors and illustrators on our website: www.franceslincoln.com